Henry White

**In praise thereof and other pieces in rhyme**

Henry White

**In praise thereof and other pieces in rhyme**

ISBN/EAN: 9783337271084

Printed in Europe, USA, Canada, Australia, Japan

Cover: Foto ©Andreas Hilbeck / pixelio.de

More available books at **www.hansebooks.com**

# IN PRAISE THEREOF,

# AND OTHER

# PIECES IN RHYME.

BY

HENRY J. WHITE.

BOSTON.

FRANK K. FOSTER, PUBLISHER.

1897.

*Now, if one could but choose the way,*
    *And loiter through with scraps of song,*
*Could pluck the doubtings that delay;*
    *Then one were wise with life, and strong.*
*Oh, well, indeed, if souls were so,*
    *Life would not all so strangely seem;*
*A something dominant—a dream.*
        *One then could like the day and night,*
*Hope, love and laugh, and graveward go*
        *Within the compass of delight.*

*How oft I of these themes have sung,*
    *And likewise have I stood in thought*
*Till my poor vanity is stung*
    *That wisdom is so deftly wrought;*
*As I, too many sadly know*
    *That life is an uncertain shift;*
*I and the millions have no thrift,*
    *No saving days of grace have we,*
*'Tis take your crosses up and go*
        *Till some sweet angel pleads for thee.*

*Now, if I croon a pretty song,*
*    Or tell in rhyme a passioned thing,*
*Unless all spent with life and wrong*
*    You, too, shall know the muse I bring,*
*Life songs, and songs of drift, and more;*
*    Mood to the rhyme turned fancy-wise—*
*You have them: half the singing lies*
*    With whoso listens, and today*
*A singer offers from his store*
*    Songs gathered, crooned, along the way.*

# DRIFT.

Drip and splash of rain,
  All night long;
Dreams of loss and gain,
  And bits of song.

Hour by hour the night
  Dragged thus away.
Oh, how I hailed the light
  At break of day!

Moods and measures strange
  Entangle me;
I drift, and starless range
  On land and sea.

Drifting here and there,
Spying my way;
But night is everywhere,
As well as day.

Drip and splash of rain;
Utterly spent
In dreams of loss and gain
The long night went.

# MY RIVER.

The quaint old line, I croon it,
  It comes so musingly —
" Our lives are little rivers
  With longings for the sea."

My river, too, went winding
  Through field and vale and mead ;
Its strength was love with courage
  For some chivalric deed.

It reached the mighty ocean,
  Was swept out on the sea,—
Was lost with love's last kindness
  In its immensity.

And 'mid a million rivers
Obscurely mingling there,
My river is forever lost,—
God only knoweth where.

# GROPING.

Groping, like a blinded beast!
    Strange that it should come to pass
God's decree should have a king
    Grope among the leaves and grass.

Scorn for shame now, that a king
    Should be stung by folly, thus;
A foolish fable it must be,
    That has drifted down to us.

Bowed, brown back and long, dun beard,
    Calloused hands and knees; and he,
Scarred and wet and mud-defiled,
    Silent as a stagnant sea.

Some mad poet's bitter jest,
 Seems it all; and yet, perhaps,
This uncleanly king did grope
 To escape more gross mishaps.

Yet it stings us to the quick,
 Gazing on a grovelling king.
Well! and yet hath our own day
 Witnessed many a sadder thing.

# IN PRAISE THEREOF.

God be praised for what we have,—
    God be praised, I say;
A crust to eat, a clout to wear,
    The promise of another day.
God's goodness fills me full with prayer,—
    God be praised, I say;
The devil is driven to despair
    And God is king, today.

Last year we had no song to sing,—
    God be praised, I say;
The wolves that followed us last year
    Are nowhere to be seen today.
Oh, life had basely grown severe,—
    God be praised, I say;
The wolves that filled our soul with fear
    Are dead and gone today.

Ah, hunger is a wolfish thing,—
    God be praised, I say;
I hear no constant cry for bread,
    There are no hungry ones today.
The word goes forth that want is dead,—
    God be praised, I say;
I saw two children in their bed,—
    Both died of want today.

God be praised for what we have,—
    God be praised, I say;
That you and I may sing a song,
    May live and hope another day.
Only these children? It was wrong,—
    God be praised, I say;
He took them where sweet things belong,
    They're safe with Him today.

# ALAS !

Sick of it all, and O !
    Whistling to kill care.
What is the good ?
Quiz, quiz, quiz,—
    And never an answer anywhere.

Weeks and months and years,
    Common old ruts, and I :
Just lumbering on.
Jog, jog, jog,—
    And so till the day we die.

Gad, and heigh-ho, me.
    Stretched out on the grass,
What a blue sky !
Well, well, well,
    God, too, must say, Alas !

# SKY AND SEA.

A low sky, brooding, like a sullen thing,
    (The absolute murmur of the sea,)
And a shrill wind
    That eats into the very soul of me;
Marsh hens skim above the grass,
    And boys at play
Shout, leap and dash along the road
    That hems the bay.

The wind is keener than a whetted knife,
    And the dull sky, brooding there,
Compels an instant fellowship
    With duller care.
But the glad boys are trooping on,
    Little to them is drear,
And in some deep recess of grass
    The marsh hens disappear.

## SKY AND SEA.

Dusk, and brooding over sea,
    Black and deep gray
Night comes, a petulant passion
    To despairing day ;
And I, to lone ways trained and in accord
    With what may be,
Stroll on, exulting in the gloom
    Of sky and sea.

# IN HER EYES.

Dimly foreshadowing
    Throes that shall be;
Her eye-depths revealing
    Soul-fancies, and she
Anxious and beautiful,
    Petulant and sad,
Strives 'gainst disaster —
    Every nerve in her glad
At love's expression;
    Lawlessness there —
Her eye-depths foreshadowing
    Love's weakness, despair.

God might control her;
　　Men but allure.
Soul too susceptible,
　　But she is pure.
Sad her inheritance,
　　Pity who may,—
When she's a soul wreck,
　　Passionate clay,—
Past all controlling,
　　Hate in her eyes;
And in that sweet soul
　　What blasphemy lies.
She, now behold her,
　　Saintly, serene,
Unconscious of passion
　　As a child in a dream.

There, quickly turning,
　　A vulgar half-word
Deems you impertinent,

Something is stirred —
A sense of injustice
Probing one so,
Whose soul-depths reveal more
  Than strangers should know.
Superb and dainty,
  Who shall it be
To first gain admission
  To her sanctity?
Who — may God pardon
  His sins, for I say,
Hell's gates shall open
  For the exiles that day.

# THE HANGING.

They hung him on a gallows-tree,
   Fol de rol de rol!
The minister spoke of charity,
   Fol de rol de rol!
Begged his foes to let him alone,
A pitiful object, skin and bone,—
He the fellow of passion, and he
Who stabbed to death his enemy,
   Fol de rol de rol!

'Twas worth a thousand miles to go,
   Fol de rol de rol!
To see the hanging.   What a show!
   Fol de rol de rol!

The minister after the hanging said
Never an ill word of the dead.
"A passionate fellow; walked astray;
Another passionate man did slay;"
        Fol de rol de rol!


The sentence ran, "Hang till you die;"
        Fol de rol de rol!
And every juryman did sigh,
        Fol de rol de rol!
The judge was tender-hearted, too;
Said, "May God's mercy come to you!"
Reporters and the people there
Echoed the Bench's little prayer,
        Fol de rol de rol!


His daughter had a rosy face,
        Fol de rol de rol!
That was his and her disgrace,
        Fol de rol de rol!

All of a sudden a lover came,
Clever and gross, so known to fame;—
A catcher of hearts; in making love
He knew the science well thereof,
    Fol de rol de rol!


They dallied, and the sport was rare,
    Fol de rol de rol!
Flowers and gems stuck in her hair,
    Fol de rol de rol!
Beyond all laughter it was sad;
Men gibed the father; he went mad;—
A man of moods and passions, he,
But honor bright as man could be,
    Fol de rol de rol!


They went, like fools, from bad to worse,
    Fol de rol de rol!
Pleadings, threatenings, then a curse,
    Fol de rol de rol!

A fearful oath, a terrible oath,—
And then a knife plunged into both.
Horror!  The city stood tip-toe;—
The rest of the story of course you know,
    Fol de rol de rol!

# ENOUGH SAID.

One word's enough,
    What is the use
    To pile up mountains of abuse?

Say, "Oh, the fool!"
    That's plenty said.
    Don't fling mud balls at his head.

He vexed us all,
    The fool, I say,
    And then he staggered in the way.

Some one jeered,
      And down he went,
      Mire and muck and what contempt?

He raved and swore,
      Blasphemed, too;
      Till every nerve was tingling through.

Let the rest go!
      What is the use?
      He's dead, and past feeling abuse.

# FOUL PLAY.

Foul play; alas,
  Cock Robin is dead
And the sparrows are twittering
  Over his head.

There's a man whose soul
  Was as white as snow,
But he dyed it black
  An hour ago.

"Foul play," he cried;
  And the bean-stalk grew
Up to the sky,
  Children tell you.

The man in the moon
     Looks on and sees
Fate's nimble fingers
     Run over the keys;


And the tune she plays
     Glad children sing;
But grown men laugh
     At everything.


" Foul play," he said,
     As they laid him down,
But there wasn't a fool
     Like him in town.


For his white soul,
     Marble and pure,
Was, if ever soul was,
     Firm and secure.

But a sweet face,
   Blue eyes, and hair
Like threads of gold
   And love sighs, there.


Men laughed, and fate
   Lingered awhile —
To bury Cock Robin
   We walked a mile.


Sunset, and then,
   Oh, then? O! she
Strained a soul out
   Of his body.


Life's a thing rare,
   Mother Goose old
And Boccaccio, too,
   The thing has told.

My story is done,—
   Cock Robin is dead;
And the sparrows are hopping
   Above his head.

# FAIR JUNE.

Fair June, aglow with tenderness,
   Burning with desire ;
   Flinging in her lavish way
   Fruit and flowers all the day ;
   Perfumes rising, to expire
In wanton loveliness.

Where the brooklet rounds the hill
   And the cedars lean,
   Maiden fair and wooing lad,
   Brimmed with life and soul love-mad,
   And all the world a dream,—
Be still !

Fleecy clouds adrift on high
    And youth's first love in arms ;
The brooklet ripples singingly
And the light wind clingingly,
    Soothing all alarms, —
For love is shy.


Oh, that night should come so soon !
    Only in the west
Red and gold enlace the sky,
And the soft winds gently sigh, —
    Love is gone to rest :
The loon !


Through the moistened grass they went,
    And their silence seems
Deeper than the moonless night.
Lost is something in their flight,
Something withered in their dreams.
Peace !    June is penitent.

# AIR CASTLES.

No rhyme but to some purpose, now.
 And yet I halt and muse;
Look out upon a lilac tree,
 Like one who will not choose.

Will not, because it little counts
 When aim is not intent,
And the mind, like a loiterer,
 Is past staid management.

But from the lilac's odor I
 No inspiration get;
I drum upon the window-pane,
 And whimsically fret.

Alas!!  and so the story ends ;
    My castles in the air
Are barred to entrance, and I kneel,
    Alms-asking, always, there.

## DUTY AND I.

Just to let a notion
  Have its way,
I let myself with folly
  Fool and play.

Who should meet us idling
  On the road
But duty, overburdened
  With a load?

Loaded back and shoulders.
  Folly said:
" Pile another burden
  On its head."

Folly fled and left us,—
Duty there, and I ;
And down together sat we
To laugh and cry.

# THE PLAINT OF A LONELY ONE.

She is so far away,
  I long to see her
Through the long, lonely night
  And through the day; ·
I long to see her,
  She is so far away,
And I, alone,
  Am like a fool astray,
Longing to see her.

She is so far away,
  And I so lonely
And restless grown, and sad;
  Longing, just only

To look upon her face,
To hear her speak,
So lone am I without her,
Simple and weak.

She is so far away,
I mope and yearn,
Longing for the sweet day
When she'll return ;
And every hour that goes
I hail with glee,
Knowing it nearer brings
A loved one back to me.

# THE CHANGE.

The first day we met?
The change is so great,
It seems like a dream wherein one has no state.
I marked that your eyes were brilliant and jet;
Your carriage and gait
Enamoured my soul, led me slave unto thee,
I loved and I knelt; you gave love to me,—
The first day we met,
O fate! O fate!

Well, curse then the day!
And so we must part?
That love should such poison instil in one's
heart!

Or was it not love, but a passion's wild play,
    A poisoned love-dart?
My soul flew, white-winged, to thee in delight,
Your kisses came burning my soul in its flight.
      Well, curse then the day,
    And its art, – its art.


      Ah, the change is so great,
    And, alas! we must part.
The charm is down-broken, love lies in the
    mart;
Passion's adrift like a thing of no state,
    A love-haunting hate.
Well, a song for the dream. I'll rhyme it,—and
    yet
' Twas sweet, was it not? the first day we met?
    Dear heart! Dear heart!

# YESTERDAY.

"Why, Yesterday lies dead,"
  Cries, gaily, glib To-day,
"And the To-morrow lies afar,
  A million hopes away."

.

Why, Yesterday and I
  Were one a while ago ;
I loved a maid, we crossed our hands,
  And dallied to and fro.

Her sweet words are yet
  As music in my ears ;—
"Shall we not wed to-morrow, love?"
  "Yes," whispered she, in tears.

" But Yesterday lies dead,"
    Again breathes low, To-day:
" And on the morrow shall you wed
    The maiden, as you say?"

Why, no! The dream is past;
    For that was years ago;
Yet, oh, it seemed but yesterday
    We dallied to and fro!

Aye! that was but a dream,—
    By the folly of dream misled.
For she, with all my yesterdays,
    And better things, lies dead.

"What, then, of brave To-morrow?"
    To-day did softly sigh.
"Oh, it may be to-morrow, sir,
    I with my love shall lie."

# POISON.

Poison ?   That's rare !
  What can it be?
I sip the stuff
  And it ends me.

True,—what you say !
  Life's just a sip.
And death is what
  Upon the lip?

There! hold it up,—
  I hate the stuff;
Life's short, and art?—
  Aye, that's enough.

One grain ?   Ah, well,
    Just make it two !
Then, half and half,—
    What say ?—with you ?


Agreed, then,—here goes !
    Old world, to-day,—
God !   But it stings !
    There !—there !—I say !

# THE COMMON PEOPLE.

The people and the struggle, and, oh, time !
May a singer vent his feelings in rhyme ?
 The struggling common people—
In their efforts for existence are sublime.

The people !  How they welter, live and die !
The labors that they cling to patiently they try ;
 The earnest common people,
In their struggle to subdue each truth-destroy-
  ing lie.

The people !  Oh, the wayward !  All sincere,
In their splendid, earnest struggle, year and
  year ;
 The thoughtful common people,
In their steady onward movement have no fear.

The people! Oh, the masses, here and there;
Those who labor and yet suffer, children born
     of care;
   The eager common people,
Rich in knowledge are of life that comes from
     long despair.

The people! List, the people! They would
     speak.
Patience all is broken, they are dangerously
     meek,
   The waiting common people,
In their struggle tell to each the reason they
     are weak.

The people! Oh, the dreamers and the wise!
Telling tales prophetic of a future grand sun-
     rise,
   The restless common people,
Breaking bars of thraldom for the promised
     prize.

The people! Oh, the failures and the gain!
Bread and substance wasted for a victory of
  pain;
  The honest, common people,
Take it to their aching hearts with armor on
  again.


The people! Oh, the weary, lacking art!
Lacking deeper knowledge, taking wisdom
  from the heart;
  The calloused common people
In their struggle for existence demand an
  equal part.


The people! Oh, the watchword time will
  tell!
There's a bitterness in failure that will jest
  with sin and hell;
  The wretched common people
Know it, feel it, and will teach it, too, as well.

The people! Oh, the people! Well-a-day!
The singer to his bent has had his say;
  The merry, common people,
Yet shall fill the world with laughter and be
  gay.

# ON THE BEAT.

Say, policeman, you can answer
  Any question one may give?
I surmise that you can answer
  How most men and women live.
On your beat, around the corners,
  Up and down the market place,
If your eyes are good for seeing
More than when a rogue is fleeing,
Surely you have strange adventures
  With a section of your race.

What? "You don't take much stock in
  People who go on their way?"
Still, I'll wager you take stock in
  Some, and more or less each day?
Good! That's right! Only, I wonder,
  Since your trade is to observe,

That you do not probe and sound it—
Human nature—and expound it,
Just for pastime, or say knowledge,
   That a fellow would preserve.


"Guess work all, and sometime easy
   When the case is in your hand."
Wise policeman !  " Guess work's easy,"
   Eh ! you say, " I understand."
Go no deeper.  Right good fellows
   Get fooled badly, too alert.
Probing, guessing, for a clue to
Something that they're devilish new to,
Think they know, but flounder only,
   Like boys playing in the dirt.


Gad!  You have upon your shoulders
   Something can be termed a head ;
What we find on most men's shoulders
   Gets some other name instead.

I'm not laughing! No, policeman,
  You impress me just so much;
Yours is a brain to what your trade is,
Know life where the light and shade is,
Don't get muddled over problems
  That no man of sense would touch.


Well! But, then, what's human folly?
  That's a thing you comprehend.
Don't you rub 'gainst human folly
  From day's dawning to its end?
Men and women in its practise,
  Aren't they thriving on your beat?
Tell the truth! You must be wise, there.
Say! policeman, with your eyes there,
Don't you see much sad tom-fooling
  Everywhere in house and street?


"That's all right! Man's only human!"
  Ah, the clue have I at last.

"It's all right, for men are human?"
   Well! Well! Well! The die is cast.
Dear God! And, I say, policeman,
   Folly is then condoned for that?
It's hard teaching, and its uses
Means, go gently with abuses?
"No!" You firmly contradict me,
   Blest if I'm not beaten flat.

Ah, you've got the upper hand, now.
   Where policeman drew the line
Folly gets the upper hand, now.
   Human nature's whittled fine.
Men and women,—so much matter
   Touched a-through, of course you hold,
With a grace that saves; a soul-life
That completes and makes a whole life
Of the merely mortal human,—
   Am I stating it too bold?

No! You jibe in with my saying,

It's not mine; I only draw
Inference from your own saying,
   You take stock in such a law.
"Too deep are we?" That is folly.
   Well, policeman, let us rise,
On your rounds you oft beat into
Men and women, to whom sin to
Is just simply second nature,
   God's own hand-work, I surmise.


What! That's blasphemy? God's pity!
   You and I are damned, if so,
Past all pardon? Dear! God's pity
   Reaches infinitely low;
May reach us—ah, what's the matter?
   Startled! We are all adrift.
Take it so, policeman! Take it!
Life is as God and man make it;
Go much deeper, we get muddled,
   Therefore let the subject shift.

Still, I think, oh, wise policeman !
　　You've the best chance of us all,
Just to watch what the world's doing,
　　As men and women rise and fall.
I but wished to quiz a little,
　　That's my weakness, and I play
On it as men thrum a fiddle,
Or as children with a riddle,—
Thank you, I am glad I met you.
　　Here's the sergeant, too. Good day !

# IN GETHSEMANE.

In Gethsemane no favors went
  But of high grace, and sweet accord
Men gathered there.  No malcontent
  Followed the footsteps our Lord.
Remembering what the place had been,
  So holy, by His presence fair,
Sorrow to tutor to every one
  At last is goddess there.


In Gethsemane who laughs shall fail.
  Laughter within that sacred place
Means sin, and yet not sighs prevail,
  But men and women in disgrace
And 'mong the trees in hiding there,
  Weak and unhappy as can be,
Men slack and faint, and women, too,
  On knees to sorrow constantly,

In Gethsemane! Oh, tale and song,
  And jest, and, too, sweet prayer is heard.
Not as when He got from the throng
  For love of death, had whispered word
Next went, and unattended He
  But by the rabble vile and glad,
Who jested at the Cross, and then
  Were stricken and made sad.


In Gethsemane! And the years go,
  Life's sorrows still are harbored there,
Spite of what men complete or know.
  The Cross is still a load to bear.
And, so, for lack of other thing
  This Easter Eve, so sad am I,
And full of love for Him whom men
  Left hanging on a Cross to die.

# HURT.

Hurt! And you know it.
Bruised! And you say :
" Better luck next time :—
Some other day."

Waiting? What patience!
Whistling for luck.
Hurt, and it pricks you,
Toughens your pluck.

So, and the end comes,
You stumble and fall.
That's the whole story.—
God knows it all.

# BY-GONES.

We talked of foolish by-gones,
  A dozen of us there;
"I wonder," at last, a fellow exclaimed,
  "If the devil doesn't care

"When a soul comes tumbling to him,
  Pell-mell and in despair?
I wonder if, after all," he cried,
  "If the devil doesn't care?"

So much abject sorrow,
  Souls, souls, from everywhere,
Exiled from heaven. "I wonder, indeed,
  If the devil doesn't care."

# FLATTERY.

You could not flatter him, and say,
　Spite of all failure it was grand
To hold one's own in such a fray,
　Though beaten,—well, you understand?

He simply veiled his eyes.  No word
　To such drear flattery he gave.
The prating touched him, you inferred,—
　The wise, and silent, too, and brave.

Beaten!—That is the story all,
　Spite of the fight he made to rise;
Beaten!  Yet in his own downfall
　He scorned your flattery and lies.

# THE HOUSE ON THE SAND.

I've built my house upon the sand,
  Let wind and wave do what they will,
My house is built upon the sand,—
  Oh, wavering heart, be still!
My house is built of reeds and dreams,
And held together by sunbeams,
The sills are of the rarest schemes,
And my house, built upon the sand,
Till Judgment Day shall stand.

Oh, wind and wave, what is your will?
Brave heart, be still!
We're shielded by the roof of hope,
To sky and sea our windows ope,
  And light comes in from everywhere.

My house is built upon the sand,
  And hall and room are furnished rare;
Wealth was so fluent in my hand.

What's wealth, unless you spend it so?
Behold! as through my halls you go,
  The lavish treatment and the art,
The sense of sweet security
  In every part.

I built my house upon the sand;
I might have chosen firmer land;
Have laid stout timbers, too, I say,
And built of brick, or stone, or clay.
But what's the use? Nothing shall stay,—
This, ah, we understand,
Therefore I built upon the sand.
  Laughed, but my heart went pit-a-pat,
And fools and wiser folks did glare;
The whole world looked upon me there,—
  I did not wince at that.

One's house is what one's soul can be,
　　One's soul is its o wn shelter, too;
So I went on contentedly
And built upon the sands.　And you?
Your house is built of stiffer stuff,
Of timber seasoned well, and tough.
I do not wonder you are shy,
And at me stare and hasten by;
　　But I've a sweet advantage, too,
My house upon the sand shall stand
　　Till Judgment Day is due.


Come, spend an idle hour with me!
　　The doors are always open there;
　　Strangers drift in from everywhere,
To talk and muse, and be
　　Men of the world, who do not care
What special honors come to thee.
Good fellows, always, half a score,
Oft times, and oft that number more,

Who love to linger and to spend
An hour with things they comprehend.


Oh, but the wind is never still;
  You always hear the sea waves lash;
I laugh, and you say what you will,
  My house shall never go to smash.


The timbers bend, and sing, and sway,
The sills shift twenty times a day;
In every room the whistling breeze
Are to me like piano keys,
Played by unseen and skilful hands,
Sweet nocturne of the shifting sands;
And at night, when I lay me down,
I would not change my lot to be
The czar of all the world; no frown
Disturbs the dreams that come to me..
And thus from day to day I go,
God, and the angels, too, I know,

Care for my house upon the sand.
Therefore, forever it shall stand,
And I, forever living there,
Cry out, Old World, I do not care,
I've built a house upon the sand,
That till sweet Judgment Day shall stand.

# GUESS WORK.

It's just the merest guess work,
   What's the best thing to do,
Knowing that failure is stalking
   In grim pursuit of you.

Failing, the work grown heavy,
   You falter and grow stale;
Collapse, and then give up the job,
   Escaping to weep and rail.

Strange words, and sad confusion,
   And a little while you stray ;
Utterly routed, at last you go,
   Glad to be laid away.

# AN OLD TRUTH.

Ah, me, I know,
   Because, forsooth,
   It's an old truth,
We reap just as we sow.

And this old thing,
   For centuries long
   Has been a song
For all mankind to sing.

And men grow wise,
   When, at the end,
   They comprehend
The wealth that in this saying lies.

And I just cling
To this old truth,
Because, forsooth,
'Tis something every man may sing.

# STRANDED.

It was not fair to load her,
  So slightly built was she,
With freight no stout three-master
  Could carry easily.

Knowing her frail condition,
  Shame on you, stevedore,
To overfreight and send her
  Chartless, away from shore.

Lo, she is gone to pieces,
  Keeled up against the town;
Wrecked, and her precious cargo,
  Soul and all, gone down.

# THE SINNERS.

Helping sullen sinners?
Lend a helping hand,
Just to make it evident
What you understand

Of the drift about you.
They, the sinners, oh,
Laugh at your endeavors,
Fooling with them so.

They, and you, and Satan,
They've got learning, too.
All by heart, and sadly.
Wiser far than you,

Sullen sinners, helpless,—
What's the use? I fear
You and I but waste our time
Preaching sermons here.

# MAUD,—KATE,—NELL.

Gowned and painted and glad,
  Off for a night is she,—
Maud,— or Kate,— or Nell,—
  Whatever her name may be,—
Gowned and painted and glad,
  Ready for you or for me.

Eager for life, and, I say,
  Sinking her soul in excess,
What in the world does she care
  What sensitive ones profess ?
Eager for life, and, I say,
  To joy in its bitterness.

Knowledge she has that you
  Never can understand ;
Wheedles and teaches you all,
  With the turn of her head or her hand ;
Knowledge she has that you
  Or money cannot command.


Fools you up to your eyes ;
  Wins and juggles your heart,
Tramples it under feet,—
  The vulgar little upstart !
Fools you up to your eyes,
  Playing with consummate art.


Pity her ?  Pity who can,
  When she is off for a night ;
Sinking her soul, as I said,
  In every forbidden delight.
Pity her ?  Pity who can,
  By standards of wrong or of right.

Nell,— or Katie,— or Maud,—
  Whatever your name may be,—
The world is no better than you,
  With all its hypocrisy.
Nell,— or Katie,— or Maud,—
  I'm doffing my hat to thee.

# FROM DAY TO DAY.

From day to day,
From year to year,
And on until our last adieu,
Our lives go trailing round and round ;
We have our say,—
A laugh, a tear,—
And then, beneath a little mound,
Lies all that is of me and you.

We act and dream,
We sigh and hope ;
And all the while our fate's at hand.
We guess, grow wise, we doubt and pause,
And every scheme within our scope

Doth rise and fall at some command
Beyond the reach of human laws.


Let's have our song,—
Live, love and die ;
Bid fate seem nobler than a god ;
And when it knocks upon the door,
We'll join the throng
Without a sigh,
But bravely, as stout fellows shod
To travel on forevermore.


All ways are mine ;
And you, dear soul,
Stand fearless, when the knock is heard.
O women, men, and comrades all !
The glow divine
Is to control
One rounded moment at the fall,
To welcome in the final word.

High lights for life,
For man and beast ;
Love, honor, truth, and passion, too ;
Baseness abjure, from folly fly,
    And mid the strife prepare a feast,—
For you may be the next to die,
And, who knows, I may follow you.

# SHE ANSWERS BACK.

Oh, that's my trade and I don't care;
  The old world laughs and so do I;
The stuff to get is coin, and there
  I let no golden moments fly.
        So let me be!
  You waste your time preaching to me.


I don't go fishing in the dark;
  Aren't looking half one's life ahead;
Nor working for reward, or mark,—
  That may come when I'm with the dead.
        I show my hand,
  That you at once may understand.

Life is all right, and after that,—
  Well, after that, and there you are !
It's just a childish bit of chat.
  You stoop too low or reach too far,
      Just as you fail
To hold me with a Bible tale.


My trade, perhaps, sticks in your crop?
  Hurts ? Yes, that such a trade should be
Not built like yours, pillar and prop,
  For white-winged angels sweet to see.
      Yes, sir, I know
There's something else behind the show.


I don't talk wanton and don't boast;
  That's vile and common. I just sell
The goods I deal in for the most
  Cold cash, and let the rest go. Well,
      Ah ! What ! Your eyes
Are bulging with a painted surprise?

I'm woman? Yes! On that you preach,
  You're kind to talk of my poor soul
As something Christ Himself would reach,
  But how, or when? Who'll pay the toll,
    Good fellow, say!
  You've booked more than you ought to play.


I don't mean to talk back, or cheap;
  I like you, and am glad you call.
But, if I can't vent sighs and weep,
  Its just because I can't — that's all.
    Times were — but, oh,
  That was years, and years ago.


Now let me be! That's the best way.
  You've got me thinking! There's a clue,
Come up my street some other day
  When you have nothing else to do.
    You know the place!
  And don't mind who laughs in your face.

# IN THE QUICKSAND.

We buckled to our work,
It was, Pitch in! Never shirk!
Half the town was loafing there.
Boss was ripping mad.   He'd swear,
   Every other word a curse.
Sweat was pouring down our faces.
It was fearful, it was fearful!
Women, men and children tearful,
   Nothing could be worse.
Every accident disgraces
Men or man who know their places.
Eighteen diggers buried in
   By the caving of a trench,
By the breaking of a brace,
   By a sand-slide and a wrench,

Eighteen diggers buried in
Thirty foot of sand.
  Every worker straining through,
  Just as I am telling you,
  Tried to save if possible an humble life or
    two.
In an hour sixty men,
Used up, were laid off, and then
Sixty fresher men were there,
Digging like fiends in despair,
And all day they shifted, shifted;
Oh, the tons of sand were lifted,
  With men to relieve and stay,
  Giving up at each relay.
And the boss was hoarse from driving,
Utterly used up, contriving;
No one like him; ought to know.
Eighteen dead men lay below,
Eighteen laborers below.
Slowly down we got the digging,

Got beneath the hoisting rigging,
   Got the lower set of timber,
   Heavy, stiff, but as lathes limber
'Neath the pressure of the sand,
The treacherous quicksand,
Stuff no fool should handle,
Takes a man to understand.
   And the news, it filled the papers;
   Such reports, they cut such capers.
It was funny after reading
With their praise for us all, pleading,
And they told the story rightly
Of the find that was unsightly;
   Of the horror that ran through us;
   For a time it did undo us.
Read the papers! They will tell you,
For a cent or two they'll sell you,
Such a story, how, the Boss said:
" Every damned one of them is dead!"
   Eighteen diggers dead below,

In the quicksand there below.
Bruised by timbers, battered, fearful,
Children, men and women tearful,
Every mother's son is dead,
"God Almighty !" The boss said,
" Every mother's son in dead !"
    Then he leaned against a brace,
    Something awful is his face,
Eyes were dull as lead,
And he staggered, then, and over
With the eighteen others, dead.

# LOSING HER WAY.

Simply lost her way,
  Wandered up and down,
And everybody saw her
  Coming into town.

Everybody laughing
  That she lost her way;
But she kept on, blindly,
  Fearfully asking.

No one would direct her,
  And she wondered why;
Then, in desperation,
  She began to cry.

Louder grew the laughter,
   Then perplexed her so,—
Then a fatal misstep,
   And every one said, "Oh !"

Beaten out completely,
   Down, oh, down, went she,
And the merry folks who laughed at her
   Are laughing now at me.

# WAITING.

Waiting!
    Oh what sorrow and hating
    Comes from waiting;
    People languishing in sorrow
    Sighing, " Change shall come to-morrow,
    Just by waiting."

Waiting!
    Sighing for the change and hating
    This sad waiting;
    Life's so sad, and 'mid the sorrow
    Men cry, "Change will come to-morrow.
    Just by waiting."

Waiting!
    Children, men and women, hating
    So much waiting;

Beaten out and lost in sorrow,
Wail, "This pain must end to-morrow,
    Just by waiting."

Waiting !
    Millions groping blindly, hating
    All this waiting,
Cry, "The world's place of sorrow,
Maybe death shall come to-morrow,
    Just by waiting."

Waiting !
    Men and women, tired of hating
    And of waiting,
Wrap themselves up in their sorrow,
Crieth, "There is no to-morrow,
Nothing but a prolonged sorrow !"
    Waiting, waiting.

# A CONFESSION.

Slipped from my bearings a moment!
  Pity, oh, pity is rare;
Intellect must be weakening,
  Kneeling was I in prayer.

Half ashamed to confess it!
  Fifty odd years ago
Mother would kneel beside me,
  Whispering low

Words of praise and prayers,
  Christ's goodness and help and hope.
" Darling ! My boy," and there, now,
  You may measure my scope.

Eh! but, alas, I outgrew her;
  Got away from her strings;
Lived a man's life, forgetting
  A thousand beautiful things.

Never forgot her a moment,
  Only her prayers, and such,
Mingling with other barbarians
  Lost their meaning and touch.

Older now, but no wiser,
  Age only consumes one's wit;
But lonely, and foolish, and longing
  Far more than I'll ever admit.

So down on my knees I tumbled,
  Something gave way, and a sigh
That my mother were kneeling beside me,
  Dear God! What a child am I?

# THE WHISTLER.

That's for folly, and I whistle
　　Like a fool who doesn't care.
Laugh and pile the burdens on me,
　　Pluck to do, and you I dare.
That's my trade, and so I whistle
　　As I lug the load along,
Folly's just a sad fool-getter,
　　And I whistle out the song.

Well, and so, and, hallo, fellows!
　　I shall keep the common way.
Can't a fellow play his whistle
　　Who has not a word to say?
I look not nor crave for favors ;
　　Time was when I did, but, oh,
That was when I was a youngster,
　　Years and years and years ago.

Older now, and so I whistle;
  The devil is always in the play,
I have seen a million soul-wrecks
  So, good fool, out of the way!
Glad to whistle, though my burdens
  Callous every limb of me.
What's the use to prate 'gainst failure,
  Unless one loves misery?

So for folly, boon companion,
  Many a day to me, and night,
I just pucker mouth and whistle,
  Desperate, to a fool's delight,
All the same, the hurt goes deeper,—
  But no word of that, and so
Thankful that God's mercy's certain,
  Whistling down the road I go.

# AMONG THE WRECKAGE.

Hail, you fellow, with swollen eyes,
  Tangled, wet hair and a bruised face,
What brought thee to this dismal state?
Who stamped on you that look of hate?
  "Storm winds," Ah? That's no disgrace
Only one shuns its enterprise.

A jovial song, I crave thee, sing,
  Though curses end the chorus, yet
No joy's complete till sullen woe
Drags from stout heart what waves forego.
  A wave-washed corpse one may forget,
But a love-wrecked heart is a bitter thing.

Hail, ho! fellows! A corpse is here,
  Beaten and blown and bruised to death;

Waves and winds are hard to stay,
Ships and souls were in the way
    A sea-lash whipped him out of breath
And wrecked the vessel and all her gear.


Wert thou a fellow of jest and song?
    Or wert thou solemn and worldly wise?
Lift him over the spar, ah, see
His bruised right hand is clutched, maybe
    Looking old death straight in the eyes,
Hailed him fighting, bold and strong.


Man—what is man to wind or wave?
    Ah, say, ask that dead fellow now!
    He lived how many eager years,
    Aspired, and sighed? I think, somehow,
    We'd better dig for him a grave
And take on trust what best appears.

# THE FOOL SAID.

The fool said :
  " I will be wise,
On steps of past experience
  My work shall rise."

The fool said :
  " I shall be great;
I know why Caesar failed.
  I hold my fate."

The fool said :
  " My way is sure;
I comprehend and feel
  I shall endure."

And when they buried him
A priest said:
" Ashes to dust again!"
This when they buried him
A priest said.

# A JUNE DAY.

A June day, and the wind
  In mood as quiet and as free
As will of maid to whom
  Love steals on suddenly.

A fragrance in the air ;
  And robin — a bird to know —
Pipes, as you cross the field,
  A few notes, sweet and low.

Well ! and a June day !  Rare
  To loiter along, and just
Man enough in oneself
  To question the theory of dust.

Sweet June, and Robin, and I,
  And the wind to make a song ;
A superior person, indeed,—
  Thus easily jogging along.

# SULLEN AND HURT.

Sullen and hurt!
   What is to be done?
Move out of the light,—
   He's in need of the sun.
Let him lie there,
   The devil may care,
And nobody else,
   For a thing in the dirt.

It injures one so,
   Seing a man
So utterly wretched,
   Under the ban,
What can one do?
Appealing to you
   Is folly, and nonsense,
And whimsical, too.

Only, right here,
  As he went down,
What a broad grin
  All over the town !
We, every one,
  Said he would fall.
    Bellowed and laughed
At the climax of all.


  Well, we were right !
    Slumping he went,
God !  What a pity !
    Used up and spent.
Let him lie there,
    Sullen and hurt,
Genius and folly
    A-sprawl in the dirt.

# IN THE SKY.

The news spread fast like fire,—
   "Hallo! Hallo! Behold!
A million artists in the sky
   Are painting red and gold!

On tip-toe stood the world,
   The wondrous sight to see,—
So many artists, so inspired
   To splendid tracery.

Night of a sudden came,
   And, gleaming in the sky,
A golden crescent,—such a work!
   A million artists sigh.

# AH, WELL!

We know not and we grumble.
  "Ah, well!" a fellow said,
"Let us pray God He give us
  Wisdom as well as bread."

We stray about and stumble,—
  Yet light is everywhere,
Only our eyes are blinded,
  Facing, so long, despair.

And at the end so humble
  Upon our knees we fall,—
"Christ! Saviour! Brother!—Help us!
  We need Thee, one and all."

# ALONG THE BEACH.

The winds are at play to-night,
  The blue waves whine and lash,
The pale moon's quivering light
On the crest of each wave is bright,
  And weird as a lightning flash.

The moon hath veiled her face,
  A frail, fair maiden in fear ;
And mist, like moistened lace,
Clings to the threatening place,
  And the sobbing of the surf is drear.

Cries loud, and fierce, and bold,
  Come bellowing over the sea,
And dirges from depths untold
Of purposeless sorrows that hold
  Life and eternity.

Shriller the north wind blows ;
   The mad waves speed to its call,
Each crested thing bestows
The might that in frenzy grows,
   When the elements would appall.

The pale moon is crept away
   Back from the face of the earth,
And the lightning's vivid play
Illumes but a moment, to betray
   The utter extinction of mirth.

# THE WORST OF IT.

"What a sad fellow!"
  You said, as he went
Moping along,
  In discontent.

It was sadness, indeed,
  To note and trace
As you looked for a while
  In his whimsical face.

You wondered, and said,
  "What can it be
That tortures that fellow
  So drearily?"

And this one thing
  All his friends say,
" A woman ! a woman ! "
  Whom he met one day,

Who fooled him awhile.
  Now, he's on the town,—
And she, like the others,
  Is laughing him down.

## SAYINGS.

" Everything comes to the waiter ;"
    And a whimsical fellow said,
" Funerals, funerals, funerals !
    Everywhere some one dead."


" Patience will bring a crowning ;
    And a man, about to die,
Turned to the wall and murmured,
    "There are graves in the sky."


A girl who fell on the pavement
    Was never again the same,
And her children are blind as fools
    And as cripples lame.

And so it goes on forever,
  And the whimsical fellow said,
" Funerals, funerals, funerals!
  And the living to bury the dead."

# QUATRAINS.

## I.

One more glass ! And to his lips
   The baneful stuff he sips and sips,
Then like a brutish thing he lay,
   Sprawled on the floor, till dawn of day.

## II.

Now summer days are at an end,
   And scarlet leaves are in the air,
"Tis time for you and me, dear friend,
   To say our beads,— our souls prepare.

## III.

To know one's self were a drear thing indeed.
Therefore, my earnest friend, I pray take heed
Lest this self-knowledge humble thee and show
How frail a soul, forsooth, you come to know.

## IV.

The tempter came, with sweet persuasion rare,
The stripling list and, too, the maiden fair.
But a fine sense of loveliness came, too,
Hence all their lives they have been lovers true.

# LOST.

Kept right along
   Till some one said,
" Look out ! Beware !
   Danger ahead !"

I saw red lights
   Flash in the air,
And I said, " That's so !
   Danger lies there."

Turned back, and went
   Another way.
Since then, I am like
   A fool astray.

Danger ahead !—
The fellow he lied,
The road was clear
To walk or ride.

And the red lights
I saw flash there
Were a trick of the devil
To lure and snare.

But astray so long
I can never retrace,
So I keep on plodding
In a sullen pace.

Hoping some day,
White lights shall show
Before death comes
The road to go.

## ALONG THE ROAD.

Dust, and discontent, and rot,
　　And murmurings all along the way ;
God ! What a dazed and shiftless lot ?
Men and women, who rot and rot,
　　And are dismally estray.

The wind laughs bitterly in each face,
　　And every whipped-out victim there
Cries out, " Oh, God, we lacketh grace ! "
The tears scald down each iron face
　　Hard as despair.

The daisies by the roadside weep,
  The birds are dumb, and every tree
A sombre monument to keep
The ghosts of souls, that wail and weep,
  And tease hell constantly.


And down the dusty, flinty road,
  Souls of things both sweet and foul ;
And overhead, in the blue sky,
Ravens and hawks and vultures fly ;
  And the wolves prowl,
Snarling at souls that lie and die
  On the dusty road.

## FIDDLE, AND DOG, AND I.

Fiddle, and dog, and I !
  Worth a nickel, I say ;
Isn't it worth a nickel, sir,
  To hear me play ?
Strings for fiddle to buy,
Doggie must have a bone,
And I,—
  Well ! Say !
Isn't it worth a nickel, sir,
  To hear me play ?

What is your favorite air ?
  Whistle a bar,—I'll play.
Doggie shall dance a nickel's worth,
  Just as you say.
Nickels will buy us bread,

Fiddle strings, too, and a bone.
I said,
What shall I play?
A nickel ain't much for a banker, sir.
To give away.

Dog, and fiddle, and I,
Gathering nickels. so;
If every day were a pleasant day,
We'd like it, you know.
But snow, and rain, and sleet,
And hunger,—once in a while,
The street. .
Dog, fiddle and I,
Ah! many a night have we
Just played to the sky.

Give us a nickel! What?
The E string's lacking tone;
Don't you see that my dog

Needs a bone?
And I, my fingers are numb,
Slipping along the strings.
But come!—
    A dollar!   Hello!
God reigns! You're a gentleman, sir,
    I know.


Fiddle, and dog, and I,
    Never again complain;
What is the use?  You're a gentleman, sir!
    I maintain
A lover of art.   Ah, me!
Success is turning my head.
Come, dog!   Good bye!
Art never shall die
While generous gentlemen live.
Your hand, I say,
Come, dog!
Good day!

# SONG.

Soul's delight is song,—
  A singer of sad, sweet, sullen themes;
Down where the brook and cedars are
  Facing the sea in dreams.
Marvelous beauty there,
  Blue sky, and sea, and mood,
For souls to a song delight and joys
  Of solitude.
Songs for the moment ripe,
  The grass and the path to the brook
  And never a cranny or rook
But a songster is hidden with pipe.
  Soul's pain and body's ease,

And merry of tune and sad,
　　And melodies,
Till the soul's a-dream in song,
　　Forgetful of things that be ;
God only knows, of longings adrift,
　　To the blue sky and the sea.

www.ingramcontent.com/pod-product-compliance
Lightning Source LLC
Chambersburg PA
CBHW032103010726
47493CB00008B/2508